Thoughts
Journaled
by

_____

Taking Time for Tea
JOURNAL

~

Published by Harvest House Publishers
Eugene, Oregon 97402

Cover design featuring art by Sandy Lynam Clough
taken from *If Teacups Could Talk*
by Emilie Barnes

For information regarding the cover art, titled "Tea Time," contact:
Sandy Clough Studios
25 Trail Road
Marietta, GA 30064

Designed by Garborg Design Works, Minneapolis, Minnesota

_With clearer eyes one looks through this amber well at truth,
and rises hope-refreshed._
ANONYMOUS

_____

_____

_____

_____

_____

_____

_____

_____

_____

_____

_____

_____

_____

_____

_____

_____

_____

_____

∽

Although my neighbors are all barbarians,
And you, you are a thousand miles away,
There are always two cups on my table.
TANG DYNASTY (618-906 A.D.)

~

*My dear, if you could give me a cup of tea to clear my muddle
of a head I should better understand your affairs.*

CHARLES DICKENS

I love things that bear the touch of time, chips and all—
they're more beautiful than perfection.

BALLERINA QUOTED IN _VICTORIA_ MAGAZINE

The daintiness and yet elegance of a china teacup focuses one
to be gentle, to think warmly and to feel close.
CAROL AND MALCOLM COHEN

~

*"I can just imagine myself sitting down at the head of the table
and pouring out the tea," said Anne, shutting her eyes ecstatically.
"And asking Diana if she takes sugar! I know she doesn't but
of course I'll ask her just as if I don't know."*

LUCY MAUD MONTGOMERY, ANNE OF GREEN GABLES

*What part of confidante has that poor teapot played ever since
the kindly plant was introduced among us.*

WILLIAM MAKEPEACE THACKERAY

Come and share a pot of tea,
My home is warm and my friendship's free.
A N O N Y M O U S

_____

_____

_____

_____

_____

_____

_____

_____

_____

_____

_____

_____

_____

_____

_____

_____

_____

∽

Tea quenches tears and thirst.

JEANINE LARMOTH AND
CHARLOTTE TURGEON